Ling

Maddy

Alphonse

Harry

Claudia

Vikram

Georgia

Archie

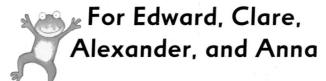

For Edward, Clare, Alexander, and Anna

Copyright © 1999 by Zita Newcome

First U.S. edition 1999

Library of Congress Cataloging-in-Publication Data

Newcome, Zita.
Animal fun / Zita Newcome.—1st U.S. ed.
p.   cm.—(Toddlerobics)
Summary: A group of toddlers has fun imitating a penguin, a crab, a duck, an
elephant, and other animals while they exercise.
ISBN 0-7636-0803-3
[1. Exercise—Fiction. 2. Toddlers—Fiction. 3. Stories in rhyme.]   I. Title. II. Series.
PZ8.3.N44 An   1999
[E]—dc21   98-42390

2 4 6 8 10 9 7 5 3 1

Printed in Hong Kong

This book was typeset in Arta Medium.
The pictures were done in pencil and liquid watercolor.

Candlewick Press
2067 Massachusetts Avenue
Cambridge, Massachusetts 02140

Toddlerobics
Animal Fun

Zita Newcome

CANDLEWICK PRESS
CAMBRIDGE, MASSACHUSETTS

Give yourself a jiggle, come join in—

Animal Fun is about to begin!

Waddle like a penguin from side to side—

Flip your fins—imagine you're a fish!

back straight, arms down, feet out wide.

Swim through the sea with a splish, splash, splish!

Scuttle
like a crab
on your feet
and hands.

Thisaway,
thataway,
across
the sands.

Hands can be starfish —

stretch fingers wide.

Now floating jellyfish,

swirling in the tide.

Quack
like a duck
and
bend down low.

Move
your elbows
to and fro.

Squat
like a frog,
flick your
tongue in the sky.

Jump
right up and
catch that fly!

Be a kangaroo!
Go hop, hop, hop!

Swing your arms like a monkey in a tree.

Whoop and scratch and jump with glee!

Stomp like an elephant,

Circle round the room with a

lift that trunk.

thump, thump, thump!

Put hands together, make a hissing snake.

Gallop like a horse, give your mane a shake!

Flutter
your
wings,
be a
butterfly.

Swoop
down low,
then
soar up
high.

Lie on your tummy,

wriggle like a worm.

Roll and writhe,

twist and squirm.

Take deep
breaths

as you lie
on the ground.

Sssshh!
Curl up

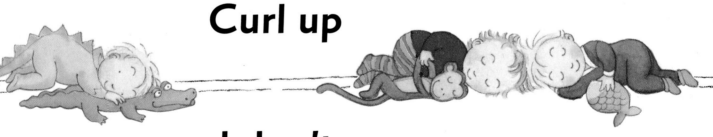

and don't
make a sound.

That was GREAT!

Let's all take a bow.

Toddlerobics is fun
when you know how!

Ling

Maddy

Alphonse

Harry

Claudia

Vikram

Georgia

Archie